BY M. SOBEL SPIRN
ILLUSTRATED BY KELLEY CUNNINGHAM

Librarian Reviewer
Marci Peschke
Librarian, Dallas Independent School District
MA Education Reading Specialist, Stephen F. Austin State University
Learning Resources Endorsement, Texas Women's University

Reading Consultant
Mark DeYoung
Classroom Teacher, Edina Public Schools, MN
BA in Elementary Education, Central College
MS in Curriculum & Instruction, University of MN

STONE ARCH BOOKS
Minneapolis San Diego

Vortex Books are published by Stone Arch Books,
A Capstone Imprint
1710 Roe Crest Drive
North Mankato, Minnesota 56003
www.capstonepub.com

Library of Congress Cataloging-in-Publication Data
Spirn, Michele.

Poison Plate / by M. Sobel Spirn; illustrated by Kelley
Cunningham.

p. cm. — (Vortex Books)

Summary: When Mark first becomes the foster child of
restaurant owners, he thinks they just want free help, but when he is
wrongfully accused of trying to sabotage the business he is determined
to find the true culprit.

ISBN-13: 978-1-59889-069-3 (hardcover)

ISBN-10: 1-59889-069-7 (hardcover)

ISBN-13: 978-1-59889-280-2 (paperback)

ISBN-10: 1-59889-280-0 (paperback)

[1. Restaurants—Fiction. 2. Foster home care—Fiction. 3.
Orphans —Fiction. 4. Mystery and detective stories.] I. Cunningham,
Kelley, 1963–, ill. II. Title. III. Series.
PZ7.S757Poi 2007
[Fic]—dc22   2006007682

Art Director: Heather Kindseth
Graphic Designer: Kay Fraser

Photo Credits
Karon Dubke, cover images

Printed in China.
092015
009240R

TABLE OF CONTENTS

THE  NEW SLAVE

Twelve-year-old Mark Thomas sat in the front seat of a strange car and stared out the window.

"You're lucky," Ms. Owens said. She took one hand off the steering wheel and brushed her hair behind her ears. "Sometimes it takes a long time to find the perfect family."

Perfect? thought Mark. Yeah right. Nobody's perfect.

"Why can't I live in my old apartment?" Mark asked.

"I understand it's hard to leave," Ms. Owens said. "But your apartment will have someone new living in it by next week. You're too young to live alone. And you've got no other family."

"What about Mrs. Berk?" asked Mark.

"I know she was your neighbor for a long time, Mark, but she's not a relative." Ms. Owens turned and smiled at Mark. "Don't worry. The Morrises are very nice. You'll like them."

Ms. Owens talked some more, but Mark wasn't listening. He was trying to pretend this wasn't happening.

Mark didn't want to leave his home, but he didn't have a choice. It had all happened so fast. Mark remembered running across the hall and pounding on Mrs. Berk's apartment door, shouting that his mother was sick.

He remembered the men from the ambulance running up the stairs and pushing past him. He remembered the police officers pulling him away from his mother as she was carried out by the ambulence workers. He remembered meeting Ms. Owens. She had been holding a stack of papers and asked him lots of questions.

The car stopped.

"This is it," said Ms. Owens cheerily.

They had stopped outside a small white house with red shutters and a red door. The house was surrounded by a trim, green lawn with hedges on either side. A pot of yellow flowers sat on the front steps.

Mark noticed there were no tall buildings nearby. Instead, next to the house was a restaurant, also painted red and white. A big sign over the door said 'Red's.'

Ms. Owens led Mark up the front steps of the house and rang the doorbell.

Mark wanted to run. Every event that happened in his life was worse than the last. Years ago, his father had become sick and died. A few weeks ago, his mother had died from a heart attack. Now he had to meet new people and live with them. What if these people didn't like him? What if he didn't like them?

The door opened, and a tall man with red hair greeted them with a smile. He reminded Mark of a friendly, red bear.

"We've been waiting for you," said the man. He held out his hand. Mark shook it and let it go fast.

"I'm Red," he said, motioning them to come in. "Red Morris. You must be Mark."

Mark nodded and looked around.

The living room was filled with old chairs and a big sofa. The smell of something delicious hung in the air.

"Let me give you some papers to sign and then I'll be on my way," Ms. Owens said to Red.

"Bring anything with you, Mark?" Red asked.

Mark thought of all his clothes and games and books that he had left behind. Where were they now?

"Mrs. Berk packed up all your things," said Ms. Owens. "We're sending them over."

Just then, a woman bustled out of the kitchen.

"Hi, Mark," she said. "I'm Della." Della was much shorter than her husband. She was round and plump, and her hair was the color of butter.

"Are you hungry?" Della asked. "I've got some soup and sandwiches for lunch, and cookies, too."

"Wait until you eat Della's food," Red said. "Your stomach will smile."

Della led Mark into the kitchen while Red signed Ms. Owens's papers. Yellow flowers, like the ones outside on the front steps, sat in vases by the kitchen window. The room smelled like a Thanksgiving dinner.

Mark took a seat at a small table and watched as Della spooned out the chicken soup.

"Here you go," said Della. The soup smelled delicious. Mark ate it up greedily.

"Have a cheese sandwich," said Della.

Mark took a bite and made a face. It didn't taste like the cheese his mother used.

"Different, isn't it?" Della said. "It's a special kind of cheese from Italy. We use it in the restaurant. Anything left over we eat at home."

"The restaurant belongs to you?" Mark asked.

"Didn't Ms. Owens tell you?" said Della. "The restaurant is our baby. Along with our son, Tim, of course."

Mark didn't know there would be another boy in the house. "How old is Tim?" he asked.

"Tim's thirteen, and he's a real help in the restaurant," Della said. "Red is teaching him how to cook."

Mark's mother had done all the cooking in their kitchen. "Isn't cooking for girls?" he asked.

"Of course not," said Red, stepping into the kitchen.

He sat down, then went on. "Some of the greatest cooks in the world are men. Cooking is a real art."

A timer on the oven started ringing. "I almost forgot," Della said. She leaned down and opened the oven, pulling out a sheet of chocolate chip cookies. The smell made Mark hungry again.

Red reached for one, but Della slapped his hand playfully. "Now, Red, you know better than that. Let them cool."

"Cookies!" said a new voice. The kitchen door swung open and in walked a tall, skinny boy with red hair, a younger, thinner version of Red. The boy looked at Mark for a moment and then turned to his father.

"This the new kid?" the boy asked.

"Yes, Tim," said Della. "Please say hello."

"Hi," said Tim, looking at the cookies.

"Why don't you take Mark upstairs," said Red. "I'd like you to show him the room you two will be sharing."

"Cookie first?" Tim asked.

"Room first, cookie after," said Red.

Tim turned, walked out of the kitchen, and started up a set of stairs. Mark followed him. Maybe Red and Della would be okay, but he wasn't sure he was going to like Tim.

Tim stopped at a door with a sign posted on it: Keep Out! This Means You.

Tim opened the door and pointed to a bed on the far side of the room.

Mark looked around. All of Tim's things were neatly put away. His books filled one shelf and his games were stacked on another. A small TV sat in the corner. Tim's clothes were squeezed into one side of the closet.

The other side was empty, probably waiting for Mark's things.

Mark felt as if his old bedroom was a million miles away. His stomach felt as empty as his half of Tim's closet.

Tim stood in the center of the room and looked at Mark. "Listen up," he said. "We're not going to be friends. If my mother and father want you here, that's fine. If we have to work together in the restaurant, okay. But stay out of my life."

"I didn't ask to come here," Mark said. "And I don't want to be here. As for working in the restaurant, count me out. That's not my job."

"We'll see about that," Tim said. He threw himself on his bed, turned on the TV, and clicked through the channels until he found a baseball game.

Mark didn't move.

He had wondered why the Morris family wanted to take in another kid. Now he knew the answer. They wanted someone to work for them without pay. He would be their new slave.

CHAPTER TWO

NO  GOING BACK

Returning to the kitchen, Mark found Della mixing more cookie dough. Red was drinking a cup of coffee. "Everything okay?" Red asked.

Mark shrugged.

Della smiled. "I have a feeling you two boys are going to be good friends."

"We're all going over to the restaurant," Red said. "I should have been there hours ago. But I wanted to stay home so that I could welcome you."

"Am I supposed to work there?" Mark asked.

Della and Red looked at each other. "We do things together," Red said. "That's what makes us a family."

"During the week, you and Tim need to do your homework," said Della. "But on Saturdays and Sundays, you can help out a little in the restaurant."

Mark frowned.

Red called upstairs to Tim. "Let's go, buddy. Time for a little work."

"It doesn't take us long to get to work," Red joked.

Della opened the back door next to the refrigerator. A few steps led them across a short cement sidewalk to another door. This door opened into the restaurant.

The restaurant's main room was decorated in bright yellow. It must be Della's favorite color, thought Mark.

Small tables crowded the floor. A row of cozy booths lined one wall. Two of the booths were filled with customers.

"Saturday lunch isn't so busy," said Della, "but everybody comes for dinner."

A small man in a white apron shuffled over to Red. "Just wanted to warn you, boss. Marilyn's in a bad mood," he said.

Red put his arm around Mark.

"Sidney, this is Mark. He's going to be living with us," he said.

"Pleased to meet you, kid." Sidney smoothed down the little hair he had. He stuck out a big hand for Mark to shake.

"Sidney's our best waiter," Red said.

"Kid, I'm the only waiter." Sidney grinned and walked toward the booths.

"I'll have a chat with Marilyn," Della said.

"No, I'll talk to her," Red said. "I know what she wants. More money."

Sidney called Tim over to one of the booths. "Tim, I could use your help."

Red and Della walked toward the kitchen at the back of the restaurant. As Mark followed them, he saw a tall, blond teenager wiping some glasses.

"That's Lucas," Red said. "He brings people water, bread, and butter. He sets up the tables, too. I'll introduce you after I'm done speaking with Marilyn."

In the kitchen, the air was hot. A large woman was bent over an oven. When she stood up, Mark could tell she was angry.

The woman had gray hair pulled back from her face, and an apron was tied tightly around her plump middle.

"The pot roast is fit to eat tonight," she said. "So are the mashed potatoes, no thanks to anyone but me." She put her hands on her hips.

"Sorry, Marilyn," said Della. "We were next door with our new friend."

"Mark," said Red, "say hello to the best cook in the state. No, in the United States."

"No point in buttering me up, Red," Marilyn said. "I need more money. I'm worth more money. And if I don't get more money, I'm out the door. I can always work for Grant at the Hungry Bear — you know that."

Red led Marilyn away from the oven. "Let's talk about this, Marilyn," he said. Red and his cook walked out of the room. Della started peeling carrots and slicing tomatoes.

Suddenly a skinny man poked his head inside the kitchen door. He had curly black hair and blinked at Mark though a pair of thick glasses. "Della, we need a few more coffee cups. Some of them broke while I was washing them," he said.

"Okay, Bert," Della said. "By the way, this is Mark, the new person in our family."

Mark liked the way she said it.

"Pleased to meet you," said Bert, looking down at his feet. "I'm the dishwasher here. 'Water, water, everywhere, nor any drop to drink.'" With that, he slipped away.

Mark looked at Della. Della smiled.

"He's a good dishwasher," she said, "and a very shy and gentle person."

Marilyn and Red came back into the room. Marilyn was laughing.

"I'll make it up to you soon, Marilyn," Red said. "We're on this month's list for Martin Simon, the food critic at the *Times*."

"You're kidding!" Marilyn exclaimed.

"One of my friends at the paper told me. And when Simon writes about how great our food is, we'll be packed every night!"

"I'll be ready for him," said Marilyn. "No one makes a better prime rib than I do. Just watch out I don't quit before he comes."

Red patted Mark's shoulder. "I'll show you your first assignment."

Out in the dining room, Tim was standing next to Lucas, wiping some forks. "Here's another helper," Red said.

"Cool," said Lucas. He handed Mark some napkins to fold.

Mark began to fold the napkins.

"You're doing it wrong," Tim said.

"So stop complaining and show him how to fold them," said Lucas.

"Total waste of time," said Tim. "He doesn't look smart enough."

Mark hurled the napkins in Tim's face. "You're so smart? Fold them yourself! I never asked to come here anyway. All your family wants is a slave."

Mark ran out the side door. Then he stopped. Which way should he go? He didn't know this neighborhood.

He stood there, staring at the door that led back into Della's yellow kitchen.

The restaurant door swung open behind him. It was the big, friendly bear.

"What's going on?" asked Red.

"I don't want to be here," Mark said. "You can find another slave."

Red looked hurt. "That's not why we asked you to come."

"You need someone to work, someone you don't have to pay," said Mark.

"Let's sit down." Red said. He patted the steps and sat down. Mark folded his arms and remained standing.

Red took a deep breath. "There were many reasons we wanted another boy in the house," he said. "Having a slave wasn't one of them. First, Della and I love kids. But we couldn't have any more children of our own. Second, Tim has been an only child his whole life. We thought it might be good for him to have a brother. Finally, we heard your story and, well, I lost my mother and father when I was young too. I know how it feels."

Mark moved his hand to the front of his sweatshirt.

"What's that?" Red asked.

Mark pulled out a chain that hung around his neck. "It's not a necklace," he said. "They're charms."

"Did your mother give you that?"

Mark nodded.

Red peered closely at the tiny gold objects: a baseball bat and a book, the two things Mark loved most. Whenever he wasn't watching baseball games on TV, he was reading.

"Mom worked in the library," said Mark.

In his old life, Mark walked to the library every day after school, did his homework at one of the big tables, and waited for his mother to finish working.

"I know how it feels, Mark. But, as hard as it is, you've got to keep moving forward."

Red stood up. "Come on. Let's get back to work."

Red was right, thought Mark. There was no going back.

CHAPTER THREE

NIGHT  VISITOR

Mark returned to help Tim and Lucas. Tim whispered, "Sorry, I was out of line before."

"No problem," said Mark. He still didn't trust Tim.

The restaurant started filling up. "Is it always this busy?" Mark asked Red as they stepped into the kitchen.

"Nah, but this is the way we'd like to see it all the time," Red said. "I like to think of it as a baseball game."

"You've got to be joking," Mark said.

"Sid is the pitcher," said Red. "He throws the orders to the catchers. That's me and Marilyn and Della. Then Lucas and Sidney run the bases. They give the food to the people. See? Just like a baseball game."

"What about Bert?" asked Mark.

"Oh, Bert's the backup. Couldn't get along without Bert," said Red.

"He seems a little different." Mark paused. He thought Bert was strange.

"Bert's okay," said Red. "Just don't ask him about what he did before he started working here. He doesn't like to talk about it."

Weird thoughts skateboarded through Mark's mind. Had Bert been a killer? A thief?

Suddenly Sidney ran into the kitchen. "Hurry it up, people! I've got folks out there turning gray waiting for food. We've got to be better than this to get a good review."

He clapped his hands. "Red, help me carry some of these plates!"

All day, Mark was too busy to think about his mother or the old apartment. The next day, Sunday, was even busier. By the time the restaurant doors were locked, and the Closed sign hung in the window, Mark could barely stand.

"You boys go on home," said Red. "Dinner is in the refrigerator. Then I want you in bed early. There's school tomorrow."

"What school do I go to now?" Mark asked.

"Tim's school," said Della. "I'll take you there tomorrow. I'll tell them you're living with us now and they'll get your old records."

The next week seemed strange to Mark. He was in a new school, with new teachers and new kids.

He was living in a strange house, sleeping in a strange bed, and eating strange new food. I can't forget my mom, he often thought to himself as he touched the charms that hung around his neck.

* * *

One night, after Mark had been living with the Morrises for two weeks, something woke him up. He looked over at Tim's bed. Tim was sleeping, snoring like a bull moose. But Mark was used to Tim's snoring by this time. Some other noise woke him up. His stomach?

Mark wondered if his new job gave him a bigger appetite. Maybe if he went down to the kitchen, he could find something to eat. Quietly, Mark walked down the stairs. He was used to big-city sounds: sirens wailing, people shouting, car radios thumping. But he wasn't used to the sounds of an unfamiliar house.

Mark jumped. What was that hum? He was afraid to breathe. Moving carefully, he felt for the kitchen light and snapped it on. Then he chuckled to himself. The hum was the refrigerator. As he walked toward it, he glanced out the window.

Strange. There was a light on in the restaurant. Mark looked at the big kitchen clock. Three a.m. It was too late for Red and Della to be working. Mark stood there, his hand still on the refrigerator handle.

Then he heard a scraping sound coming from the restaurant. That was the noise that had woken him up. Should he investigate?

If something was going on in the restaurant, Red and Della would want to know. Mark opened the back door and stepped out.

The cement was cold under his bare feet.

The light was still on as Mark neared the restaurant's side window. He ducked down and then raised his head to look through the window. The light went out. The restaurant grew dark. Someone had seen him!

I better get Red, thought Mark. He'll take care of this. Mark took one last glance at the window. No one there. And no one at the restaurant door.

Mark took two quick steps across the walkway. A dark figure raced out of the restaurant door and threw something white and powdery in Mark's face. Mark coughed and rubbed his eyes.

He was blind.

He was alone in the dark with a stranger, and he couldn't see!

CHAPTER FOUR

THE CLUE  OF THE RED ROCK

Mark heard the sound of breaking glass. Then he fell to the ground, yelling. His shoulders scraped against the cement. He couldn't open his eyes.

"What's the matter?" Mark heard Red's voice.

"I can't see!" Mark cried. "I can't open my eyes!"

Red's hands swept lightly over Mark's face and eyes. "It's okay, son," he said. "It's only flour."

Red brushed the flour away from Mark's eyes. The boy opened them to see Red and Tim standing over him.

"What happened? What are you doing out here?" Red asked.

"I saw a light on in the restaurant. I thought maybe someone was trying to steal from you," Mark said.

"I'll check it out," said Tim.

"You'll do nothing of the sort," his father said. "You stay with Mark. I'll go and see if it's safe."

The boys watched Red walk into the restaurant. Then Tim looked down at Mark.

"You haven't even been here a month and already there's trouble," Tim said.

Mark wondered where Red was. It had only been a few seconds, but it felt like years.

"I don't see anything wrong," Red said stepping back outside, "except a flour mess on the floor and a broken window. You boys go back and get some sleep. I'll fix the window and put a new lock on the door tomorrow."

"There was someone there," Mark said. "I know I saw someone."

"Maybe it was a homeless person looking for something to eat," Red said. "That's happened before."

Della met them at the door, clutching a baseball bat in her hands.

"Is everything okay?" she asked.

"Thanks for the backup, Babe Ruth," said Red. "I've got things under control. Looks like someone broke in."

"Burglars?" asked Della.

Red nodded. "Probably," he said. "And Mark scared 'em off."

"Mark, what is wrong with your face?" Della asked.

"It's just flour. I'll wash it off," said Mark.

"Don't do that," said Della. "It'll turn into paste." She got a dry cloth and brushed his face and shoulders. "Now, everybody back to bed."

* * *

The next morning was a Saturday. When Mark entered the restaurant, he saw Red talking to an older man in coveralls.

"That lock should hold you," said the man. "And here's a few keys for you and your crew."

The man picked up a box of tools, tipped his cap, and walked out.

"So who broke into the restaurant?" asked Mark.

"Not sure," answered Red. "I don't understand it. In the past, when a homeless person broke in, there was food missing. This time nothing's missing. It's a mystery to me."

Mark walked into the kitchen.

"Maybe it's not such a mystery," Sidney was saying to Marilyn.

"What do you mean?" asked Marilyn.

"Maybe the new kid broke in. He wanted money," Sidney said.

"I never took anything in my life," Mark said.

Sidney and Marilyn spun around.

"I didn't want to be here in the first place," Mark said.

Bert piped up. "'Let he who is without sin cast the first stone.'"

Mark hadn't noticed him there. Bert was sitting quietly on a stool. He was easy to miss.

"All right, everyone," Red said, walking in. "Enough excitement for one day. Mark, today I want you to work with Sid. He'll show you what to do."

"I'm not working with him!" Mark cried. "He thinks I'm a thief."

Red glared at the waiter.

"Your new kid was the only one around last night," Sidney said. "He could have thrown flour in his own eyes."

"Not another word, Sid," said Red. "Mark, no one thinks you did it. Everybody's just got a bad case of nerves. Why don't you go help Sid in the dining room?"

In the dining room, Sid showed Mark how to pour sugar into bowls and salt and pepper into shakers.

Mark couldn't keep quiet. "You really think I tried to break in?" he asked.

"Nothing like this ever happened until you got here," said Sid.

"It was a burglar," Mark said.

"Then why didn't he take any money?" asked Sidney.

"Maybe he was after something else," said Mark.

"Nothing in a restaurant except food," said Sidney, "and some cheap silverware."

"Then maybe that's what he was after," said Mark.

Sidney gave him a look. "Stick to the sugar bowls, kid," he said.

Tim came bounding into the room. "Did you see this?" he said. He held out a large red rock. "This is what they used to break in."

"Must have got that from under your hedges next door," said Sidney.

"Where did you find that?" asked Mark.

"On the floor, where else?" answered Tim. "It was sitting in the pile of flour Dad found last night, the same flour that was all over your face."

Mark stared at the red rock. There was something strange about it. Something that did not make sense. What was it?

Sidney looked at Mark. "All I know, kid, is that whoever broke in here didn't work here."

"How do you know that?" asked Mark.

"All of us have keys," Sidney replied.

"I still wonder why nothing was taken," said Mark.

"Maybe you scared them off, Superman," said Tim.

Whoever broke in, thought Mark, had a reason. If he could figure out why, maybe he could figure out who.

"Hey, Mark! Give me a hand," Lucas shouted, walking out of the kitchen with his arms full of bread baskets. "I heard about last night," he added. "How are you?"

"Sidney thinks I did it," said Mark. "He thinks I broke in here for the money."

"And this place is rolling in cash, right?" Lucas laughed.

"Why do you think someone would break in?" asked Mark.

Lucas shrugged. "Some homeless guy was hungry. It happens."

As the dinner hour grew near, Mark was surprised to find that he was interested in watching how the staff members worked together, like Red's baseball team. Most of the time, though, Marilyn complained about the work and the pay.

"I'm going to take that Mr. Grant up on his offer and go work at the Hungry Bear," she would say.

"What's the Hungry Bear and who is Mr. Grant?" Mark asked Lucas.

"Grant is Red and Della's biggest competition. He owns two restaurants in town, the Hungry Bear and the Black Cat. He's always trying to get Marilyn to work for him."

"Why doesn't she go?" Mark asked.

"She can't. She's got a contract with Red. If she leaves, Red can sue her," Lucas explained.

Mark wondered where Red kept his contracts. In the restaurant? A contract was worth more than food or cheap silverware.

Especially if someone wanted to get free.

 # BROTHERS?

Sidney seemed to enjoy being a troublemaker. Mark noticed that if Sidney could start a fight, he would.

Once he hid the glasses Lucas needed to set up his tables. He laughed as the teenager searched the restaurant for them.

Of the restaurant staff, Mark liked Lucas and Bert the most. Lucas was close to Mark's age and they both loved baseball. Mark liked Bert because the man was quiet and gentle.

One day Mark stopped by the restaurant after school. Red asked, "Could you get me some glasses from Bert? I need to set a few extra places."

Mark walked to the back room. He was surprised to see a stranger with white hair talking to Bert.

Mark decided to wait in the hall until the two men were finished. As he was about to turn away, Mark noticed the stranger slipping a big roll of money into Bert's hand. Mark stepped away from the doorway.

"That should take care of everything," said the stranger.

Mark backed down the hall. He watched the stranger walk toward the restroom.

Just then Red called out, "Mark, we're waiting for those glasses."

Mark stepped into the room.

"Can I please get four glasses, Bert?" asked Mark. He felt uncomfortable about the way Bert was looking at him.

"You just missed seeing my cousin, Sam," said Bert. "He's in town for a few days and he came in to say hello."

"Was that the man who walked out of here?" said Mark.

"You saw him?" asked Bert.

Mark nodded.

"Good old Sam," said Bert. "Always helping me out."

Mark wanted to ask why Sam was always helping out Bert, but he suddenly remembered what Red had once told him: Don't ask Bert about what he did before he came here. Maybe his cousin is a spy, thought Mark.

* * *

That Friday night, Mark and Tim were eating dinner alone in the Morrises' kitchen. Della had made beef stew and mashed potatoes before heading over to prepare the restaurant for the next day. Tim had heated everything up for them.

As he ate, Tim watched the portable TV that sat on the kitchen counter. He never talked to Mark, except when they were at work together. Mark had started bringing a book to the table.

Tonight, Mark couldn't keep his mind on his book. The laughter on the TV was too loud. Mark closed the book, finished his stew, and took a bite of mashed potatoes.

"Ugh!" He spit out the potatoes across the table.

"What's the matter?" asked Tim.

Mark couldn't talk. He gulped water, trying to get rid of the sickening taste.

"Don't like the potatoes?" Tim asked.

Mark stopped. "You put something in them," he said.

"Just a little soap powder." Tim laughed.

Mark stood up. "What is your problem?" he asked.

"You're my problem. Ever since you came, things have been going bad," Tim said.

"You mean that stupid break-in last week?" Mark asked. He couldn't believe people still wanted to blame him for it.

"No, I mean that my parents really like you," said Tim.

"So what? They might like me, but they love you. You're their real son. I'm just a guest," Mark said. "I won't be here forever."

"I may not be here much longer either," said Tim. He drank his water.

"You're leaving?" asked Mark.

"Or they'll kick me out." Tim pushed his plate away. "They're not going to be too happy when I tell them I'm not going to pass English."

"What? How could you not pass English? It's easy," Mark said.

"For you it's easy," said Tim. "Not everyone gets A's in English like you. You're a real brainiac."

"My mom and I used to read a lot together," Mark said.

"You must get your brain power from her, huh?" asked Tim.

Mark was quiet. He thought about the nights in his old apartment.

"Want some mashed potatoes?" Tim asked, pointing to his own plate.

Mark eyed them.

"They're okay," said Tim. "I wouldn't put soap powder in my own food."

Mark took a forkful from Tim's plate. Then another.

"Get out your English homework," Mark said.

"Why? I can't understand it anyway," Tim said.

"Then it's a good thing you live with a brainiac, isn't it?"

POISON

"Good news, folks!" Red cried the next morning in the restaurant's kitchen. "I got a tip that Martin Simon, the food critic, is coming here tonight!" Cheers from the staff filled the room.

"Marilyn, this is your chance to show Simon what an amazing cook you are!" said Red. "Sid, I'm counting on you for excellent service. Lucas, make sure his water glass is always filled and his bread basket's never empty."

Red beamed at everyone. "We know this is the best restaurant in town. Now let's show Martin Simon that it is!"

With smiles on their faces, Red and Della buzzed around the restaurant, making sure everything was in order.

On one of his trips to the kitchen, Mark saw Sidney sticking out his chest and strutting around the kitchen. He was making fun of Red.

"There's a lot to do," Sidney said, in a bad imitation of his boss. "Marilyn, you cook your heart out and maybe you'll get a few pennies more. Lucas and Sid, you slave all day without a word of thanks."

Marilyn and Lucas laughed. Neither one was doing anything to prepare for dinner. Mark looked around. Everyone else was in the dining room getting ready.

"What's the matter with you?" Mark asked Sidney. "This is an important night for Red."

"Easy, kid," said Sidney, holding up his oversized hands. "Just having a little fun."

"That wasn't fun," said Mark. "That was mean."

"Mean? You think that's mean? I'll tell you what's mean," said Sidney. "Mean is when you have your own place and you work like a dog. Then one day, because you haven't made enough money, they take it away from you. That's mean. I was on top of the world once, kid, just like Red. I had my own restaurant, my own place. My name was out front. I was going to have the best restaurant in the world. Then it all came crashing down. Bang! Don't tell me what's mean."

Red came running in. "Martin Simon just walked in the door."

"Oh, my," said Marilyn. She got busy seasoning the meat. "Tell him there's a steak special, Sid."

Sidney straightened his shirt, adjusted his tie, and walked out of the kitchen. He glanced back at Mark. "I'll do my best, sir," he said to Red.

Mark peeked into the dining room, searching for Martin Simon. The tables were packed with customers. Mark couldn't tell which one was the food critic.

Tim swung into the kitchen. "We need more bread. Hey, Marilyn, Martin Simon is having the steak special."

"Which one is Simon?" Mark asked.

"See that back booth? He's the one in the baseball cap." Tim pointed to the man.

"I thought a food critic would be more dressed up," Mark said.

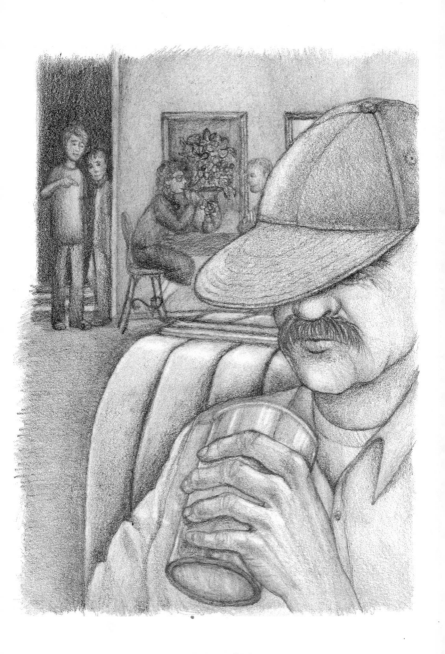

"Dad says critics don't want to be recognized. They want to blend in with the other customers. It's a good thing one of Dad's friends told him Martin Simon was coming tonight. If you just saw him, you'd never know he was one of the most important food critics in town."

"Watch out, boys," Sidney barked as he came through the doors. "This is not a good place to stand tonight."

"We don't want to miss the excitement," said Mark.

An hour later, Sidney rushed back into the kitchen. "Look at this, will you?" He waved a bunch of dollars in his hand. "That Simon guy knows how to tip."

"Did he like the meal?" Tim asked.

"Like it? He just about licked the plate clean. Marilyn, my girl, you've done it!"

Sidney grabbed Marilyn and danced her around the kitchen.

Red and Della burst into the kitchen.

"What did he say?" Red asked Sidney.

"He didn't say much, but he sure could eat. Nothing left on the plate, not even a bone!" Sidney shouted.

"Wonderful!" cried Della.

Lucas rushed in. "He's gone. What happened?"

"We've pulled it off!" shouted Red. "And if we get the kind of review I think we'll get, all of you — not only Marilyn — will get a raise!"

"Hooray!" cried Sidney.

Marilyn fanned herself with her apron, too excited to talk. Lucas and Bert smiled.

"Let's celebrate!" cried Red.

He poured some wine into glasses.

"Can we have some too?" asked Tim.

"You and Mark can toast with ginger ale," Della answered.

"We never get the good stuff," said Tim.

Red raised his glass. "To the best restaurant crew Della and I ever had!"

* * *

The next morning Mark was up early. He heard the thud of the newspaper as it landed on the steps.

Mark ran out to get the paper. He could hardly wait to open it. He looked at the headlines and then turned to the food page.

There was a photo of Martin Simon. And next to it, in big black print, the headline read: "Food Critic Poisoned."

CHAPTER SEVEN

THE SIGN  ON THE DOOR

Mark dropped the paper.

How could this happen? What would he tell the Morrises? He heard Red coming down the stairs. Mark gathered the newspaper up and returned to the house.

"What's up?" Red asked Mark. He looked so happy Mark didn't want to tell him.

"Nothing," Mark said.

"Is that the newspaper?" asked Red. "Let me see. I can't wait to read our review."

"I don't think . . ." Mark began.

"What's the matter? Is it a bad review?"
Red frowned and reached out his hand. Mark
had no choice but to give him the paper.

Red stared at the food page and groaned.
He threw the newspaper across the room and
began pacing up and down.

"This can't be true. It can't be! I've never had a case of food poisoning in my restaurant. It must be some mistake. Della!"

Della came down the stairs looking sleepy. "What is it?" she asked.

"Look at this," Red said, grabbing up the paper.

Della took it from him. She sat down slowly at the kitchen table and read the article. Then she looked up at Red. The color had drained from her face.

"This is awful," she said.

"I'm calling a meeting at the restaurant," said Red.

Tim appeared at the bottom of the stairs. "Hey, people, what's happening?" he asked.

"Martin Simon was poisoned last night," said Della.

"And it looks like the food poisoning came from our restaurant," Red said. He went off to call the rest of the staff.

"Wow! I hope the guy's okay," said Tim.

"He's in serious condition," Della said. "But what's going to happen to our restaurant?"

* * *

Half an hour later, the entire staff of Red's was gathered in the restaurant.

"I keep a clean kitchen!" Marilyn cried. "I've never had this problem before."

"Did anyone do anything differently last night?" Red asked.

They all shook their heads.

"I don't get it," said Sidney. "Why did this happen last night of all nights? Just when Simon came in!"

"I don't get it either," said Red. "It's almost like someone's out to get us."

"It sure looks like it," said Marilyn. "Normally, with food poisoning, more than just one person gets sick."

"I'll bet it was the steak," said Mark. "Simon was the only one who ate that."

"That meat was fresh," said Marilyn. "I had those steaks delivered just a few days ago."

"Maybe it's just a terrible mistake," said Della.

"Some mistake," said Red. "The only time we have trouble with food poisoning is the one night we have a food critic."

"Someone doesn't like us," said Bert.

"Who?" Lucas asked. "Besides us, who else goes into the kitchen?"

Mark didn't say anything, but he knew there had been at least two visitors to the restaurant recently.

He remembered the white-haired man who had given Bert a handful of cash.

He also thought of the stranger who had broken into the restaurant and thrown flour in his face.

* * *

The news at the restaurant only got worse. The next day a health inspector showed up on Red's steps.

He arrived early, while the staff was still preparing for the dinner rush.

"Mr. Morris, I have to look at your kitchen. Martin Simon said he got sick from eating at your restaurant," the inspector said.

"Is he going to be all right?" Red asked.

"He'll be fine," said the man, "but he's very ill. And very angry. Now, what did you serve him?"

Red listed everything Martin Simon had eaten — steak, potatoes, salad, and cake.

The inspector examined the kitchen closely. He looked at the counters, the freezers, the mixing bowl, the sinks, and the shelves of canned food. Then he took pieces of food and placed them in small plastic bags.

A section of the prime steak was the last piece of food to be gathered.

"I'll be testing these, and I'll let you know the results," said the inspector. "In the meantime, this restaurant is closed."

"Closed? I'm running a business," said Red. He pointed to the kitchen crew. "How will these people make a living?"

"I'm sorry, but we can't take any chances with people's health," the man said. "I'll get back to you with the results in two days."

"Two whole days?" cried Red.

On his way out, the inspector posted a sign on the front door.

It said, Closed by the Board of Health.

CHAPTER EIGHT

DANGEROUS MEAT

The next two days passed slowly. Red had promised to pay his staff for the days of work they had to miss.

"Think of it as a paid vacation," he'd told them.

Marilyn had cried, and everyone had hugged, but Mark had noticed that no one turned down Red's offer.

The second night, Mark helped Tim with his homework.

While they were working at the kitchen table, Tim looked up from his English textbook. He said, "I shouldn't say this, but life is a lot nicer when the restaurant isn't open. My folks pay more attention to me. Mom's here when I come home from school. I could get used to this life."

In a way, this has been a good thing for him, Mark thought. Tim had been much happier during the past couple of days.

But time dragged for Red and Della. Della spent her time in the kitchen, baking and baking until the counters and tables were overflowing with pies and cakes and cookies. Red took long walks in the afternoon.

Every time the telephone rang, the whole family jumped.

Finally the health inspector called. Red answered the phone.

"What? I can't believe it," he said. "There must be some mistake. Yes, I'll do that. Yeah, yeah, thanks." He hung up and turned to face the others.

"What did he say, Dad?" Tim asked.

"The steak we served Martin Simon was poisoned. It had bacteria, *E. coli*, all over it."

Della gasped. "People can die from that!"

"Was anything else poisoned?" asked Mark.

Red shook his head. "It's weird. The health inspector didn't find *E. coli* on anything else. All the other steaks were fine. Then he asked me if I had any enemies."

Della started to cry. She covered her face with her hands. Red sat down next to her and put his arm around her shoulders.

"Someone must have done this," said Tim.

"I don't know how," said Red. "But I'll have to let the staff go. No one will eat at our restaurant now, and I can't keep paying everyone."

"Where will they go?" asked Mark.

Della raised her head and sniffed. "My guess is they'll go to the Hungry Bear," she said. Mark remembered that the Hungry Bear had always wanted to hire Marilyn.

"They've tried to take our business away lots of times," said Tim.

"They'd be happy to get their hands on Marilyn," Della said. "Their cook is terrible. I hear he even burns the salad!" She gave a weak laugh and tried to smile.

"Will we open again?" Mark asked. He couldn't believe that in the short time he had lived with the Morrises he had come to care so much about the restaurant.

"Red's will not go under," Red said. "It will be tough, but we'll get through this together. We'll just have to work harder." He and Della looked at each other and joined hands.

"I'll work hard, Dad," said Tim.

"And I will too," said Mark.

Red smiled. "With a family like this, how can we lose?" he asked.

CHAPTER NINE

A LIST  OF SUSPECTS

The next day, Red and Della met with the staff. They waited until Tim and Mark came home from school so the boys could join them. Red explained to everyone that the meat Martin Simon ate had been poisoned.

Sidney was playing with one of the steak knives. "You should sue the meat suppliers," he said. "They're the ones who gave you the bad meat."

"But only that one steak was infected," said Red.

"Weird, isn't it?" asked Sidney.

"I think whoever broke into the restaurant last week also poisoned the meat," Red said.

"But how could they know which steak Simon was going to eat?" asked Lucas.

"The steaks weren't even in the freezer then," said Marilyn. "I just ordered those steaks a few days ago."

But Lucas had asked an important question, thought Mark. If only one steak was infected, how did that steak end up on Simon's plate?

"Seems to me," said Sidney, "that someone wants to close down Red's. But who'd want that? Not someone who depends on this place for a paycheck." He looked at Mark.

"There you go again!" said Mark. "You're always accusing me!"

"Sidney, stop right now," Red said firmly. "Mark didn't do it. And he had no reason to do it."

Della put her arm around Mark.

"Okay," said Sidney, "but don't say I didn't warn you. I think the kid will do anything he can to get out of here."

"That's not true!" shouted Mark.

Red continued, "I have to say good-bye to all of you for now. I can't continue paying you. But I hope when this place opens again, you'll all come back."

Marilyn hugged Red. "I'm sorry it worked out like this," she said.

Sidney and Lucas shook hands with Red and Della. Lucas said, "It was a good place to work."

"And it will be again," said Della.

The last one to leave was Bert, who glanced around and said, "'How the mighty are fallen.'"

He looked at Mark and said, "It's from the Bible." Then he walked out and the family was left alone in the quiet restaurant.

* * *

As the week wore on, all of Mark's free moments were spent trying to solve the puzzle. Who had poisoned the meat and why? Mark made a mental list of who could have done it.

He remembered Marilyn saying, "I want a raise. If I don't get more money, I am out of here!"

Lucas had told him that Marilyn had a contract with Red. If she walked out, Red could take her to court. Was poisoning the food critic the only way Marilyn could get out of working at Red's?

What about Sidney?

Sidney had made fun of Red.

He had lost his own restaurant and was jealous of Red. Was this his way of getting even?

Mark wasn't sure about Lucas or Bert. Why would either of them want to poison Martin Simon? For Lucas, Red's was just a way to make some extra money. He seemed to get along with everyone, although Sid bothered him at times.

Bert spent all of his time hiding in the back, washing dishes. Mark wondered if Bert even knew what food Marilyn cooked each day. Besides, Bert seemed too gentle to do something so cruel.

Then Mark remembered that white-haired stranger with the cash. Had he really been Bert's cousin?

Of course, Red and Della weren't suspects. But what about Tim?

Tim had poisoned Mark, in a way, by putting soap powder in his potatoes. And Tim was much happier with the restaurant closed.

That night, Mark lay awake in his bed. Tim was snoring. Mark was staring up at the ceiling again when he heard Della and Red talking as they passed his room.

"I'm not sure how long we can hold out," Red said.

"I know," said Della. "I'm worried about the boys. Maybe Mark would be better off with another family, a family with a stable income."

"I'd hate to see him go," Red said. "Let's see what happens."

Mark fingered the gold charms hanging from his neck. Now it was even more important for him to find the mysterious person who poisoned that meat.

CHAPTER TEN

THE  HUNGRY BEAR

The next day after school, Mark said to Tim, "I'm going to the library. I have a report to do. I'll be home later."

Tim shrugged. "Don't study too hard."

Mark walked toward the library until Tim was out of sight. Then he turned around. He headed for Union Street. After zigzagging his way for the next eight blocks, he stopped in front of a building.

He looked up at the sign.

The Hungry Bear. A neon grizzly snapped its jaws at a neon hamburger.

Mark couldn't see into the restaurant. The windows were made of dark, colored glass. He opened the heavy wooden door and stepped into a cool, dim entryway.

"Hello!" he called out.

A familiar voice called back, "We're closed until five o'clock."

Mark stepped further into the dark entryway. He could see a light shining in a nearby room.

"Hey! Didn't you hear me? I said we're closed until five," the voice said. Mark walked closer to the light.

"Well, what do you know? Marilyn, look who's here!" It was Sidney. He was sitting with Marilyn in the kitchen, just like they had done at Red's.

Marilyn was cutting up carrots. When she saw Mark, Marilyn jumped, scattering the carrots. "Mark!" She hugged him. "How are you? What are you doing here?"

"What's up, kid?" Sidney asked.

Mark shrugged. "I was just passing by. I heard you worked here. How is everything?"

"Couldn't be better," Sidney said. "Great place to work."

"This is just like old times," Marilyn said. "Let me cut you a piece of cake."

She cut Mark a big square of lemon cake and poured a cold glass of milk.

"How's Red doing?' Sidney asked.

"Okay," Mark said.

"Guess he's not such a big shot now," Sidney said. "Once you lose your restaurant, you lose a lot of friends, too."

"That's not the way it is with Red!" Mark cried.

"Sure, kid. Whatever you say," Sid said. "Take it from me. The bigger they are, the harder they fall." He grinned at Mark.

"You did it!" Mark shouted. "You poisoned the meat. You wanted Red to lose his restaurant."

"You can't say that about me," Sidney said. He picked up the knife that Marilyn had used to cut the cake. He stabbed it into the cutting board. "I never poisoned anything!"

"Sid would never do something like that," Marilyn said.

"You wanted to get out of your contract!" Mark pointed his finger at her. "Maybe the two of you did it together. It would have been easy. Sidney got the *E. coli* and you put it on the steak before you cooked it."

"You know what happens to liars like you?" said Sidney, tapping the knife in his hand.

Mark didn't wait to hear any more. He dropped his fork and heard it clattering on the floor behind him as he ran out of the restaurant.

"You spread that lie around and that'll be the last thing you do, you little brat!" Sid screamed.

Mark raced down the block. He ducked in a doorway to take a breath. He peered out and saw Sidney, the knife still in his hand, looking up and down the street.

Mark had to get home and tell Red and Della what he had learned. He was sure that Sid and Marilyn had poisoned the meat. He shivered when he thought of Sid with that knife in his hand. The waiter was more dangerous than he thought.

TRAPPED

Mark raced down the street. A few blocks away, Mark saw a taxi pull up to the curb. Bert and another man got out of the taxi.

It was the man Mark had seen in the kitchen with Bert. The man that had given Bert a lot of money.

Bert would help him, thought Mark. He would tell Bert all about Sid and Marilyn. Maybe the white-haired man had a cell phone he could use to call Red for help.

Mark trailed the men down the street. They opened the door to a building and disappeared inside. Mark stared at the sign on the building. The Black Cat. What was Bert doing here? Did he have a new job?

Mark paused. Then he thought about Sidney and the knife.

Mark opened the door to the restaurant. Like the Hungry Bear, this restaurant was cool and dark inside. He heard Bert's voice from the next room.

"Thanks for the lunch, Mr. Grant."

"Thank you," replied the other man. "If you hadn't helped me, I never could have put Morris out of business. Breaking into Red's the other night was a stroke of genius. Everyone thought it was some homeless guy looking for food. No one suspected it was an employee with a key."

Mark gulped. He moved forward into the darkness, straining to hear better. He bumped into a chair.

"Who's there?" Bert cried.

Mark began to back out of the room. He had to get out of here. He had been wrong about Marilyn and Sid. Bert had poisoned the meat. Bert, the man he had trusted.

"Who's that?" Bert came into the dark room and snapped on the light.

Mark blinked in the sudden brightness.

Bert pointed at him. "Mark! What are you doing here?"

"I was just —" Mark didn't know what to say. "You look good, a lot better than when you worked at Red's."

Bert looked down at his suit. "Yeah. I'm making more money here."

"That's great. Good for you. I guess I'll get going," Mark said, backing away from Bert.

Bert frowned. "You still didn't say what you were doing here."

Mark felt a cold emptiness at the center of his stomach. "Red told me to come over here. He said he wants you back when he opens up again."

"Fat chance," said Bert.

The white-haired man came into the room. It was the owner of the restaurant, Ray Grant. "Who's this?" he asked Bert.

"Some kid who hung around Red's," Bert said.

"Did he hear us talking?" Grant asked.

"He must have," Bert said.

"I didn't hear anything," Mark said. "I have to get home now."

"Not so fast," Grant said.

Mark moved back again, feeling for the door.

Bert reached out for Mark. "No one will ever believe you when you tell them that I poisoned the meat."

Mark ducked Bert's grasp. But he was now further away from the door.

"Why won't they believe me?" Mark asked. He was shaking.

"Who would believe a kid?" Bert asked.

"Why did you break in?" Mark said.

"Let's not call it a break-in," Bert said. "I did have a key."

"That's why you broke the window. To make it look like a stranger had broken in." That's what had bothered Mark about the red rock.

Tim had found it in the middle of the flour, but there was no flour on the rock. If the stranger had used the rock to break in, it would have been covered with flour. The rock should have been white, not red. That meant the rock was thrown after the stranger was back outside. To make it look like a break-in.

"But the meat wasn't poisoned the day of the break-in," said Mark.

"Smart boy," said Bert. "The steaks weren't there yet. But I figured if I made people believe in a burglar, no one would suspect a staff member when Simon got poisoned."

"It had to be a staff member," said Mark. "Nobody knew which steak Simon would eat until Marilyn started cooking it. It had to be one of the staff members."

"You're smart," Bert said. "But now it's over." He lunged toward Mark and grabbed his shirt.

Mark yelled for help. "Don't bother," said Bert. "No one's around. And no one's going to help you, either. Where should we put him, Mr. Grant?"

"In the cellar until tonight," Grant said.

"Then?" Bert asked.

Grant looked at Mark and smiled. "Splash."

"The lake?" Bert asked.

"I can't be linked to the poisoning," Grant said. "I can't take that chance. People will just think the kid ran away. He doesn't have any parents anyway."

The two men dragged Mark to a door in the back of the restaurant. Mark dug in his heels and tried to resist, but the grown men were too strong for him. Grant unlocked the metal door. Then they thrust Mark inside and slammed the door behind him.

"You can't do this," Mark yelled.

"That's where you're wrong. I've done a lot worse," Bert shouted from the other side of the door.

Mark shivered. "Why did you do it? Red and Della were good to you."

"Good to me?" Bert repeated.

"Red called you his backup man," Mark said.

"How much money do you think a dishwasher makes?" Bert asked. "One little job for Mr. Grant and I don't have to wash dishes for a year. I'd call that a fair trade."

"Let me go," Mark begged. "I promise not to tell anyone."

"What kind of a fool do you think I am?" Bert asked.

Mark heard the lock turn. Darkness washed over him in the cold cellar.

UNDER THE  BLACK CAT

Mark sat in the cellar and touched the gold charms around his neck. First his father had died, and then his mother. Now he was alone again. He wanted to go home.

But where was home? Back in his old apartment? Or at the Morrises' little house?

Mark thought about what had happened since Red and Della had taken him in. There had been problems with Tim, but it had been an okay place. In fact, it had been good.

Mark thought about how nice it had been to be part of a family again. He remembered how Tim had let him share his mashed potatoes. He remembered how Della had called him "the new person in the family." He thought about how Red had proudly introduced him to his employees.

Mark dried his eyes with his sweater.

It wasn't going to end like this, he thought, with him trapped like a rat in a dark cellar. He was going to get out of there somehow.

Mark looked around. He saw a faint light to his left coming from a tiny window. He piled some boxes up and stood on them. The window was too small to crawl through. A heavy, metal screen covered the glass.

Maybe there was another way out of the cellar. Mark looked around.

The cellar was crowded with boxes from floor to ceiling. The boxes were filled with canned food.

At least I won't die of hunger, Mark thought, if I can find a can opener.

Mark sat down on one of the boxes. Just then, he heard noises from above. Bert was coming back to the cellar.

Mark had only one thought in his head. He had to get away.

Where could he hide? Nothing but stupid boxes. Then he remembered a story he and his mother had read together, a mystery story about a man who hid an important piece of paper. He had hid it among other papers, so it would blend in, sort of the way Martin Simon blended in with the other customers at Red's.

Mark had a hundred places to hide.

Boxes.

Mark took a can from one of the boxes in the corner. Then he quickly dumped out the rest. He ran over to the bottom of the steps and then hid beneath the emptied box.

"I'm back!" Bert shouted as he swung the door open. Mark did not make a sound.

"Mark, where are you?" Bert called. He sounded worried.

"He's hiding somewhere," said Grant. "He won't be hard to find."

As soon as Mark heard them heading for the other end of the cellar, he reached out of the box and tossed the aluminum can as far as he could.

"He's over there!" he heard Bert yell to Grant. Just as Mark had hoped, the men ran toward the noise the can had made. Mark threw the box aside, and raced up the steps.

"Come back here!" yelled Bert.

Mark slammed the cellar door behind him and turned the lock.

"Open up!" Grant banged on the other side of the door.

"Here's a quote for you, Bert," Mark shouted. It was something his mother always said to him. "'All's well that ends well.'" Then Mark ran as fast as he could back to his new home.

CHAPTER THIRTEEN

A SECOND  CHANCE

Mark raced back home once he slipped out of the Black Cat. He told Red and Della what had happened, and what he'd found out about Bert.

Red called the police and Mark had to tell the officers everything over and over again.

Finally the police drove to the Black Cat and picked up Bert and Ray Grant.

"Those two will go away for a long, long time," said the officer.

"You won't have to worry about them again." He turned to Red. "You knew that Bert had a police record, didn't you?"

Red nodded. "Della and I thought we would give him a second chance. Who knew it would turn out like this."

"You're lucky," the officer said. "Too bad Bert didn't make the most of his second chance."

After the officer left, Red put his arm around Mark.

"Promise us you won't ever put yourself in danger like that again," said Red.

"You could have been hurt," Della said.

Tim, of course, felt differently. "That was awesome!" he told Mark. And Mark couldn't help smiling.

* * *

The next day, the health inspector returned to the restaurant.

After he left, Red called Della, Tim, and Mark into the restaurant kitchen. "Good news! We're clean and ready to open up again!"

"Hooray!" cried Della.

"Cool," said Tim.

Mark smiled from ear to ear.

"But there's something we have to do first," Red said. "Sorry, Mark, but would you wait in the dining room?"

Mark walked into the dining room and sat down. Again, he felt as if he were being left out of something.

A moment later, the Morrises came into the dining room. Della was smiling and her eyes were shining. Mark couldn't figure out what the look on Tim's face meant.

"We have something to ask you," said Red. "We took a vote and we all agreed. We'd like to adopt you and make you a real member of our family."

Mark didn't know what to say.

"Even me, if you can stand to have a brother," Tim said. "Besides, how will I ever get through English without my own personal brainiac?"

"We can never take the place of your mother," Della said. "But I think she'd like to know that you're living with people who care about you."

"What do you say?" Red asked.

Mark was hardly able to speak. He managed to croak out one word. "Yes."

Then he was folded into a huge group hug. Smells like Thanksgiving, he thought.

ABOUT THE AUTHOR

Michele Sobel Spirn started writing when she
was sixteen. She won a contest and got to go to
Washington, D.C., and meet the President. She
has always wanted to be a writer because she
loves to read and always thought that being a
writer was the best job anyone could have. She
lives with her husband in Brooklyn, New York.

ABOUT THE ILLUSTRATOR

Kelley Cunningham has wanted to be an artist
for as long as she can remember. After art school,
she worked as an advertising art director, then
went back to her first love, illustration. She has
illustrated many books for children, as well as
book covers and pieces for magazines. Kelley lives
with her three sons, Sam, Noah, and Nathaniel,
and their cat, Ivan, in Pennsylvania. In her
spare time she is an art director in children's
publishing.

 GLOSSARY

bacteria (bak-TEER-ee-uh)—microscopic living things that can cause disease

contaminate (kuhn-TAM-uh-nayt)—to make something dirty or unfit for use

contract (KON-trakt)—a legal agreement between people

critic (KRIT-ik)—someone whose job is to write a review, such as of a restaurant

E. coli (EE KOH-lye)—a bacteria that can cause sickness

inspector (in-SPEK-tur)—someone who checks or examines things

quote (KWOHT)—a sentence or short passage from a book, play, or speech that is repeated by someone else

sue (SOO)—to start a case against someone in a court of law

suspect (SUSS-pekt)—someone thought to be responsible for a crime

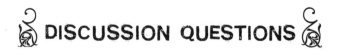

DISCUSSION QUESTIONS

1. When Mark first comes to the Morris home, Tim is not happy about Mark's arrival. He teases Mark and puts soap powder in Mark's mashed potatoes. Why do you think Tim acts the way he does?

2. When someone breaks into Red's, Sidney blames it on Mark. Why do you think Sidney suspects Mark of trying to steal from the restaurant?

3. Mark wants to find out who broke into the restaurant and who poisoned the meat. He even stays awake at night trying to solve the mystery. Why do you think he cares so much about the truth?

WRITING PROMPTS

1. At the beginning of the story, Mark does not want to leave his apartment to go live with the Morris family. He doesn't want a new home or a new family. Write about a time when you had to make a big change in your life. Were you afraid? Excited? Angry? Did your feelings change after time?

2. When Mark sees the red rock that shattered the restaurant window, he thinks that something seems odd about it. Write about a time you had a hunch about something. Did you act on your hunch? Were you right or wrong?

3. When Mark feels sad or lonely, he touches the charm necklace his mother gave him. Do you have a possession that helps you through tough times? Write about the object and explain why it is special to you.

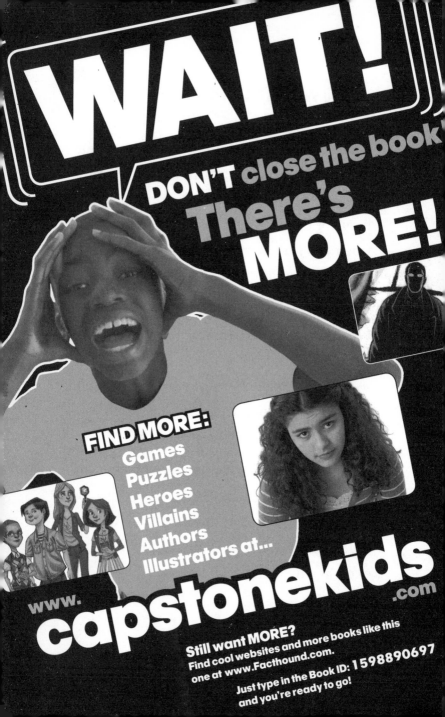